For Jamie, again

First published in Great Britain by Simon & Schuster Limited 1987
Text © 1987 Harriet Ziefert
Illustrations © 1987 Mavis Smith

British Library Cataloguing in Publication Data:
Ziefert, Harriet
Hurry Up, Jessie!
I. Title   II. Smith, Mavis
813'.54 [J]   PZ7
ISBN 0-671-65462-4

Manufactured in Singapore for Harriet Ziefert, Inc.

HURRY UP, JESSIE!

BY HARRIET ZIEFERT
AND MAVIS SMITH

SIMON & SCHUSTER

"Jessie, are you ready yet?"
Jessie's mother called from outside.

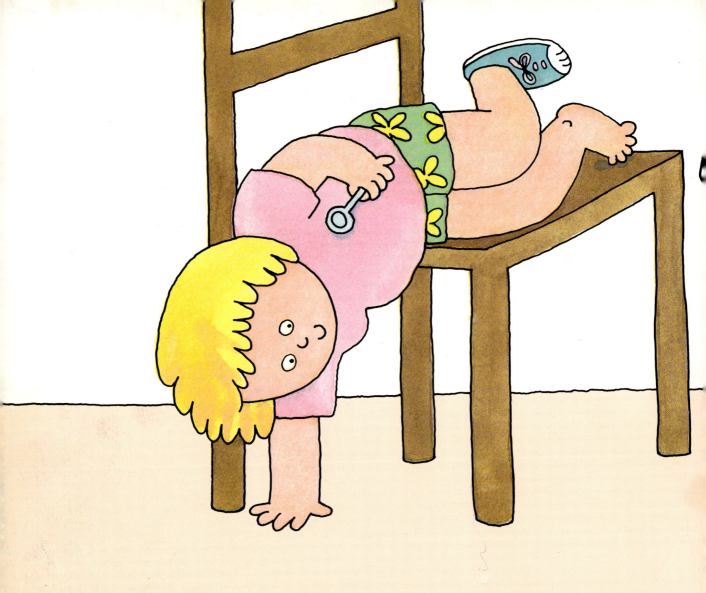

"Not yet, Mum," answered Jessie.
"I have to find my other shoe."

"Jessie, hurry up!
I want to get to the beach!"

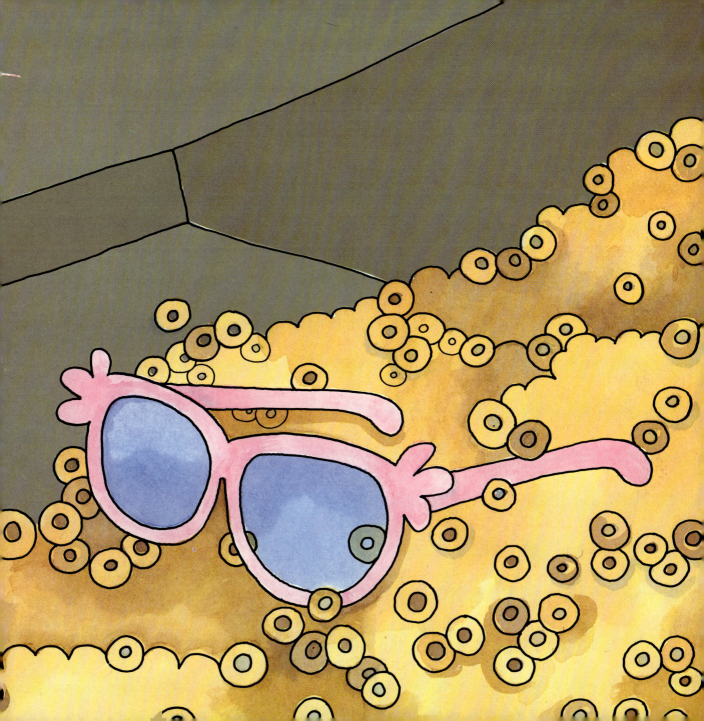

"I'm looking, Mum.
    But I still can't find my shoe."

"Please wait, Mum.
I'll be there in a minute."